THE BRUMBACK LIBRARY
OF VAN WERT COUNTY
VAN WERT, OHIO

DEMCO

◄BARBADOS►

PLACES AND PEOPLES OF THE WORLD
BARBADOS

Merle Broberg

CHELSEA HOUSE PUBLISHERS
New York • Philadelphia

Editorial Director: Rebecca Stefoff
Editor: Marian Taylor
Series Designer: Anita Noble
Designer: A. C. Simon
Production Manager: Les Kaplan
Production Assistant: Kay P. Lane
Photo Research: Marty Baldessari

Library of Congress Cataloging-In-Publication Data

Broberg, Merle.
Barbados.
Includes index.
Summary: Surveys the history, topography, people, and culture of
Barbados, with emphasis on its current economy, industry, and place in
the political world.
1. Barbados—Juvenile literature. [1. Barbados]
I. Title
F2041.B76 1988 972.98'1 87-18271
ISBN 1-55546-792-X

14.95

◄ CONTENTS ►

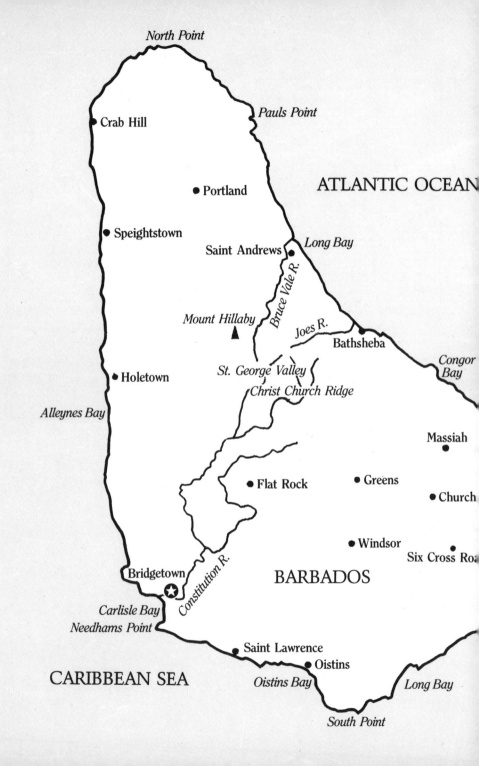

◄ FACTS AT A GLANCE ►

Land and People

Location	Approximately 207 miles (331 kilometers) northeast of Venezuela in the Atlantic Ocean; the easternmost of the West Indies islands
Area	166 square miles (432 square kilometers)
Highest Point	Mount Hillaby, 1,105 feet (332 meters)
Climate	65° to 85° Fahrenheit (18° to 30° Centigrade)
Average Annual Rainfall	60 inches (1,525 millimeters) along coast, 80 inches (2,032 mm) inland
Capital	Bridgetown
Other Major Cities	Speightstown, Holetown
Language	English
Population	252,700
Population Density	1,522 per square mile (586 per square kilometer)
Population Distribution	Rural, 33 percent; urban, 38 percent; suburban, 29 percent
Literacy Rate	97 percent
Religions	Protestant, 80 percent; Roman Catholic, 7 percent; other, 8 percent; nonreligious, 5 percent
Ethnic Groups	Black, 95 percent; white 2.5 percent; East Indian, 0.5 percent; other, 2 percent
Average Life Expectancy	Male, 67.6 years; female, 72.5 years
Infant Mortality Rate	25.1 per 1,000 live births

Economy

Major Resources	Limestone, petroleum, fish
Major Products	Electronic components, sugar, clothing, vegetables
Gross Domestic Product	U.S. $1,205,000,000
Percentage of Gross Domestic Product	Trade, 19.8 percent; mining and manufacturing, 11.8 percent; tourism, 10.4 percent; finance, insurance, and business services, 10.3 percent; transportation and communication, 8.3 percent; construction, 7 percent; agriculture, forestry, and fishing, 6.8 percent; other, 25.6 percent
Currency	Barbados dollar (equals U.S. $0.50)
Average Annual Income	U.S. $4,700

Government

Form of Government	Parliamentary democracy with a Parliament consisting of an appointed Senate and an elected House of Assembly. A prime minister heads a Cabinet of Ministers. There are no political subdivisions.
Formal Head of State	Queen of England, represented by a governor-general
Head of Government	Prime minister
Eligibility to Vote	All adults age 18 or over

◄HISTORY AT A GLANCE►

100 A.D.	Barbados is inhabited by Saladoids, agricultural Indians who make pottery.
1000 to 1500	Arawak Indians arrive on Barbados from South America. They inhabit the island until they are captured or killed by the war-like Carib Indians, a cannibalistic tribe from the western Caribbean.
1492	Christopher Columbus makes his first voyage to the West Indies. He visits several islands but does not land on Barbados.
1536	Portuguese explorer Pedro a Campo lands on Barbados, becoming the first European to record a visit to the island. He names the island, but the Portuguese do not attempt to settle Barbados.
1625	British sea captain John Powell visits Barbados.
1627	Captain Henry Powell, John's brother, brings the first English settlers to Barbados.
1628	Followers of the Earl of Carlisle arrive on the island and claim ownership for the earl.
1629	Two years after the arrival of the first settlers, 1,600 people live on Barbados.
1640s	Barbados develops a sugar economy. The large-scale importation of African slaves begins.
1642	Some followers of England's King Charles I flee the English Civil War and settle in Barbados. Many buy plots of land from small landowners and assemble large plantations.

1651	Oliver Cromwell sends an armed fleet to subdue Barbadians who pledge loyalty to King Charles II. In an agreement called the Charter of Barbados, Barbados agrees to recognize the rule of Oliver Cromwell's English Parliament in return for the right to continue its elected local government and enjoy freedom of religious expression.
1660s	Barbados accepts the rule of the English king, Charles II, and agrees to pay a 4.5 percent duty on all exports.
1700 to 1800	Preoccupied by a series of wars, England exercises little interference in Barbados's internal affairs or in its trade with other countries. Barbados participates in the triangular trade that exchanges European goods, African slaves, and Caribbean sugar and rum.
1834	The English Parliament abolishes slavery throughout the British Empire, including Barbados.
1843	Samuel Jackman Prescod, a "colored" Barbadian (a person of mixed black and white parentage), is elected to the House of Assembly.
1854	A cholera epidemic kills approximately 20,000 Barbadians.
1861	A centralized water supply system is completed in Bridgetown.
1872	International cable and telegraph service reaches Barbados.
1890s	The island's sugar economy is devastated by a price drop, a drought, an insect invasion, and a hurricane.
1942	*Bim*, a literary magazine devoted to native poetry and fiction, begins publication.
1954	Barbados's government takes on the form of a ministerial-cabinet structure. Grantley Adams becomes the first premier.

1959   Barbados's deep-water harbor begins to function, allowing large ships to load and unload directly from piers on the waterfront.

1963   Parliament extends the right to vote to all persons age 18 or more.

1966   Barbados becomes an independent country within the Commonwealth of Nations. Errol Barrow becomes the first prime minister.

1971   Sir Grantley Adams dies on November 28.

1976   Tom Adams becomes prime minister. The compulsory school age is raised from 14 to 16.

1985   Tom Adams dies on March 11.

1986   Errol Barrow wins elections and once again becomes prime minister of Barbados.

1987   Errol Barrow dies on June 1. Erskine Sandiford becomes acting prime minister.

Bridgetown, the capital of Barbados and its largest town, is a busy port.

Barbados
and the World

Barbados is one of the oldest English-speaking countries in the Western Hemisphere. A small, independent island-nation, it lies in the Atlantic Ocean, 207 miles (331 kilometers) northeast of Venezuela. Almost all (97 percent) of Barbados's more than 250,000 people, most of whom are of African descent, can read and write, making it one of the world's most literate nations. It is also one of the most densely populated, with 1,522 people per square mile (586 per square kilometer). In 1986, the last year for which figures are available, Barbadians' average yearly income was $4,700 (U.S.) per person.

Long noted for sugarcane, molasses, and rum, Barbados is now better known as a magnet for tourists. Its white sand beaches, sparkling blue water, and warm, sunny days attract hundreds of thousands of visitors.

Barbados is the easternmost island in the West Indies, the chain of Atlantic Ocean and Caribbean Sea islands that lie between North and South America. Roughly triangular, Barbados measures about 21 miles (34 kilometers) at its longest point and 14 miles (23 kilometers) at its widest. It has a total area of 166 square miles (432 square kilometers). Temperatures on the island generally range between 65° Fahrenheit (18° Centigrade) and 85° F (30° C). Barbados's location, size, and climate explain much of its history.

After Italian-born explorer Christopher Columbus first visited the Western Hemisphere in 1492, other Europeans mounted expeditions to the New World, seeking gold, silver, jewels, and slaves. Barbados, whose native Indian population had disappeared by the 16th century, had none of these treasures. Consequently, although a few Spanish and Portuguese adventurers visited the island, they established no outposts there.

The island's modern history began with the arrival of a group of British settlers in 1627. Unlike their counterparts in New England, these set-

Workers harvest sugarcane. Sugar is Barbados's main export crop.

tlers were seeking wealth, not religious freedom. Taking advantage of Barbados's perpetual warm weather, the newcomers planted tobacco, a crop that would bring good prices in Europe. Most of their workers were white indentured servants—men (and later women) who had agreed to work without pay for a period of three to seven years in return for free transportation to the New World and eventual freedom to seek their own fortunes.

The tobacco plantations were profitable, but their owners soon realized they could make even more money by planting and exporting sugar-

cane. In order to raise the new crop on a large scale, many more hands would be needed. To get them, the British planters began to import black slaves from Africa. This move would have a profound effect on Barbados's future; by the mid-20th century, most of the island's population consisted of the descendants of the men and women who arrived on its shores in chains.

Barbados's present democratic government, too, has its roots in the days of the early settlers. The island's first parliament, or law-making body, was established in 1639. At that time, it consisted of representatives elected by the white plantation owners, but after slavery was abolished in 1843, Barbados's black population began to acquire civil rights. Today's Barbadian House of Assembly is one of the world's longest-established legislative bodies.

Because most of Barbados's population is black, most of its government officials are black. The island's long tradition of representative government, however, ensures the rights of the white minority. The nation's transition from white to black control, and from colonial status to independence, occurred without violence. In a world where such change has seldom come peacefully, Barbados offers an impressive example of cooperation among people of different races and cultures.

After being a British colony for more than three centuries, Barbados became independent in 1966. It is still a member of the Commonwealth of Nations, the loose alliance of countries that were once part of the British Empire. Shortly after gaining its independence, Barbados joined the United Nations. An active participant in that organization, Barbados frequently opposes the policies of both the Soviet Union and the United States. It seeks an end to international terrorism and a better distribution of the world's wealth among developing countries. It has consistently and vigorously denounced the racist policies of the Republic of South Africa.

In 1972, Barbados helped found the Caribbean Community and Common Market (CARICOM), which develops mutually beneficial economic and cultural projects for Commonwealth nations in the Caribbean area.

One of CARICOM's successful undertakings is the University of the West Indies, a flourishing institution with campuses in Barbados, Trinidad, and Jamaica. Barbados's other international affiliations include the Organization of American States (OAS), the Pan-American Health Organization, and the World Bank.

Sugar dominated Barbados's economy for three centuries, but today it has given way to tourism as the island's main source of revenue. Sugarcane, however, remains Barbados's principal cash crop, followed by bananas and cotton. Commercial fishing is a growing enterprise, as is manufacturing. Barbados now produces and exports such goods as electrical and telecommunications components, data-processing equipment, and household appliances.

Despite the nation's booming tourist industry and the success of many of its commercial ventures, Barbados is burdened with a trade deficit. This means that, like many other nations (including the United States), it imports more than it exports. Since the start of the 1980s, its government has made a strong effort to diversify the nation's economy, encouraging petroleum production and light industry and offering favorable tax programs to manufacturers and financial institutions.

Famed for centuries as a sugar producer, currently celebrated as a tourist paradise, Barbados is perhaps even more significant for what it has demonstrated: that progress without bloodshed is possible, and that a deeply rooted tradition of democracy can endure the test of time.

The beautiful coastline of Barbados lures thousands of tourists annually.

Island in the Atlantic

When Christopher Columbus set sail from Spain on August 3, 1492, he was searching for a new, faster route to "the Indies," the fabled spice islands of Asia. Convinced that the Earth was round, he believed he could reach his goal by sailing due west. When he sighted land on October 12, he assumed he was off the coast of India. Columbus, of course, had not discovered a new route to the Indies; he had discovered a new world. Nevertheless, the name he gave the area stuck: the island chain between North and South America has been known ever since as the West Indies.

The West Indies form a 2,000-mile-long bridge between the southern tip of Florida and the northern coast of Venezuela. This bridge, or archipelago, is made up of thousands of islands, most of which are small. The West Indies' total land mass is only slightly larger than that of Idaho. Settled by men and women from Britain, the Netherlands, France, Spain, and Denmark, the islands have a wide variety of cultural backgrounds. They also have much in common: the majority of their citizens is black, descendants of African slaves imported by white settlers.

The West Indies are in the tropics (near the Equator), which means that they have almost no seasonal changes. With year-round warm weather, most of the islands have similar vegetation: coconut palms, almond trees, and brilliantly colored tropical flowers. Although the West

Indian sun is high in the daytime sky all year, its scorching rays are offset by steady northeastern winds called "the trades," or tradewinds.

Some of the West Indian islands are the tips of submerged mountain ranges, some are the result of ancient volcanic activity, and others are of marine origin, meaning that they are largely composed of ocean-produced limestone and coral. Barbados, an island of marine origin, is made up of several layers. Its base is sandstone and shale, estimated to be about 70 million years old; its central layer is limestone; and much of its surface is crusted with coral, the skeletal remains of tiny aquatic creatures. Barbados is also ringed with coral reefs.

Unlike most of its neighbors, Barbados has no sharply defined rainy season, although it receives slightly more rain from June through November than in the remaining months. About 60 inches (1,525 millimeters) of rain falls on Barbados each year. (By comparison, Alabama receives 66.98 inches, or 1,701 millimeters, per year; Arizona receives 7.05 inches, or 179 millimeters.) Rain has seeped through Barbados's limestone layer over millions of years to produce numerous caves. Rivers that flow through these underground passages provide the island with its water supply.

Barbados's highest point is just north of its center; here, Mount Hillaby rises 1,105 feet (332 meters) above sea level. West of Mount Hillaby is a series of green terraces, gently leading down to broad white beaches at the edge of the ocean. On the mountain's east side are steep hills descending to the Scotland District, rugged highlands that reminded some early settlers of the land of their birth. South of Mount Hillaby is the wide, fertile St. George Valley, the site of much of the island's best farmlands. Beyond the valley, the ground rises to Christ Church Ridge, 400 feet (122 meters) above sea level, before sloping down to the south coast. The southern beaches, along with the sandy stretches on the island's west coast, are the most popular with tourists.

Barbados's shoreline, which alternates steep, rocky cliffs with shallow, sandy beaches, offers only one natural harbor for ships. This is Carlisle Bay, an indentation on the island's west coast. Bridgetown, Barbados's capital and its largest city, is located on Carlisle Bay. Most of the island's other towns are in the south-central area, an agricultural region.

Climate

Although it is surrounded by water and lies directly beneath a blazing tropical sun, Barbados is neither uncomfortably hot nor humid. The warm trade winds, which blow all year, moderate the heat of the sun and carry off the ocean's moisture. The island's lack of dense forests also means that its air is drier than the air of many tropical islands.

Hurricanes pose a major threat in the area, especially in late summer and early fall. Many residents of the West Indies, in fact, are familiar with an old verse about these storms: "June too soon; July stand by; August don't trust; September remember; October all over." Hurricanes—intense

Like other Caribbean islands, Barbados is threatened by hurricanes every year.

Most of the fruits and vegetables that are cultivated on the island originated elsewhere.

tropical cyclones that bring torrential rain and winds of up to 75 miles (120 kilometers) per hour—regularly devastate the Caribbean region, sometimes sweeping entire villages into the ocean. Barbados has escaped most of this violent weather. It was, however, hit by severe hurricanes in 1780, 1831, and 1898. In 1955, the winds and waves produced by Hurricane Janet took several hundred lives.

Plant Life

When the first settlers arrived in Barbados in 1627, they found a profusion of brilliantly colored flowers and lush tropical plants. But the settlers had come to raise tobacco, not to admire the scenery, and they soon cleared most of the island of its native vegetation. They replaced it with tobacco and, later, with food crops they imported from South America. These included cassava, a starchy root plant still widely cultivated in Barbados; plantain, a bananalike fruit; corn, yams, and pineapples.

As the years went by, visiting sea captains added to the colonists' food supply by delivering fruits and vegetables from other far-flung British colonies. Among the crops that arrived by sea were, as an observer of the time noted, "Bonanas, Water Millions, Oranges, and Limons." Other new crops included pomegranates, kidney beans, cucumbers, and tomatoes. British ships also brought foreign trees and flowers to Barbados. Today, almost every flower, fruit, vegetable, and tree that grows on the island originated somewhere else.

From Honduras came the stately mahogany tree, whose leaves, like those of the trees found in temperate climates, turn red and yellow in the "fall"—April and May in Barbados. The tamarind, a tall, heavily branched tree that produces a pungent fruit, arrived about 1650 from the East Indian islands by way of Mexico. Australia contributed the towering casuarina, or "mile tree," which often reaches heights of 150 feet (66.5 meters). Jamaica contributed the begonia, a flowering plant that continues to thrive on Barbados. The scarlet-flowered royal poinciana (also called the flamboyant) came from Madagascar, a large island off the coast of Africa.

Many other colorful trees and flowering plants adapted themselves to the climate of Barbados, where they still flourish. Among these are the fragrant jacaranda and frangipani, the dazzling bougainvillea, the pungent ginger plant, and that bright red (but sometimes pink or white) symbol of the Christmas season, the poinsettia.

Although the early settlers destroyed most of Barbados's original vegetation, a few scattered survivors remain. Among these are the cabbage palm, whose thick, straight trunk can grow as high as 100 feet (310 meters), and the manchineel tree, which produces a tempting but highly poisonous fruit.

Botanists believe that the banyan tree, a member of the fig family, is also native to Barbados. This tree, in fact, may be responsible for the island's original name, "Los Barbados" (the bearded), which was bestowed by Portuguese explorers. Descending from the banyan's high branches are cascades of aerial roots, which could remind an observer of a bearded man.

Animal Life

Densely settled and extensively farmed, Barbados provides only a limited habitat for wild animals. The island's wildlife population consists largely of small mammals, birds, insects, and amphibians such as frogs. Green monkeys inhabit the wooded areas of the northeast, and hares and mongooses are common throughout the island. Mongooses, ferret-like hunters from India, were imported to kill the rats that once infested Barbados's sugarcane fields. The island's farmers, who no longer need the assistance of the mongooses, now regard them, along with monkeys and hares, as pests.

Amphibians abound in Barbados. Among the most numerous are tiny tree frogs, whose high-pitched whistles fill the island's night air. Small lizards, too, are much in evidence; they perch on walls inside and outside homes, quietly devouring flies and mosquitoes. Often charmed by these creatures, most tourists are considerably less enthusiastic about the island's plentiful supply of large, flying cockroaches and chigoes (sand fleas).

Barbados's domestic animals, like its plants, were introduced by early settlers. Arriving by ship were the cows, sheep, goats, pigs, and chickens whose descendants now dot the island. Some Barbadian ranchers raise substantial herds, and most country families keep at least one goat or cow tethered to a post in the yard.

Barbados is home to many species of bird. Always popular with tourists is the banana-quit, or sugar-bird. Named for its food preference—bananas, of course—this small, yellow bird can be easily lured to a windowsill or porch railing by a few grains of sugar. More imposing is the majestic frigate bird, also known as the man-o'-war bird. Although it cannot swim and can barely walk on land, this creature, which has a seven-foot (2-meter) wing span and a huge, forked tail, can cruise for hours over the ocean. It sometimes catches fish at the surface of the water, but more often, it dives at other seabirds, forcing them to give up the fish they have caught for themselves.

The pelican, another very large water bird, is distinguished by a huge, expandable pouch on the lower half of its bill. A pelican splashing into the water and scooping fish into its pouch is a sight almost guaranteed to entertain observers. One bemused pelican-watcher, American poet Dixon Merritt, recorded his impression of the creature in a limerick:

> A wonderful bird is the pelican
> His bill will hold more than his belican
> He can take in his beak
> Food enough for a week
> But I'm damned if I see how the helican.

Other winged residents of Barbados include the hummingbird, the cowbird, and the turtledove. When the weather turns cold in the North, Barbados becomes a temporary refuge for countless migratory birds. Among the island's winter visitors are swallows and sandpipers.

The waters surrounding Barbados teem with marine life. For generations, this food source was largely ignored by the islanders, who preferred to eat salted fish imported from North America. Recently, however, the commercial fishing industry has expanded, and Barbadians have begun to enjoy their abundant marine resources. Flying fish has become the nation's national dish, enthusiastically consumed by residents and visitors alike. Also popular is green dolphin—the fish, not the mammal personified by television's "Flipper." In addition, Barbadians catch and eat such native species as kingfish, barracuda, and parrot fish.

Barbadians celebrate their history and heritage during Carnival time.

A Long History

Christopher Columbus is best remembered as "the discoverer of America," but this was an honor he never claimed. Until the end of his life, in 1506, he insisted that the Caribbean islands he had found in 1492 were part of India. As the years passed, however, Europeans came to recognize this territory as a new world, one from which they might take rich profit.

In the eyes of Europe's Christians, "heathens," or non-Christians, had no rights of possession. Operating under the so-called right of discovery, European explorers felt free to claim any "heathen" land they "discovered," whether the occupants of that land agreed or not. First to exercise this "right" in the New World were explorers from Spain, where the arts of navigation and shipbuilding had been developing rapidly. More and more Spanish ships arrived in the Caribbean; by 1540, Spanish settlements were established on most of the area's larger islands.

Although the Spanish explorers paid little attention to the small eastern islands of the West Indies, historians believe that in 1518 a Spanish ship captain visited Barbados, where he captured and enslaved a group of Indians. But when Pedro a Campo, a Portuguese explorer, landed on the island less than two decades later, he found it uninhabited. When the British arrived in 1626, they, too, reported no human inhabitants. Who had lived there, and where had they gone?

To this day, no one is quite sure. In recent years archeologists (scientists who study early civilizations) have uncovered fragments of ancient pottery apparently made between the first century A.D. and about 1000 A.D., thought to be the work of a people known as Saladoids who may have been wiped out by invading Arawak Indians from South America. Archeologists believe that the Arawaks remained on Barbados until approximately 1500, when they were driven away or killed by new invaders.

Taking over from the Arawaks were the Carib Indians, for whom the Caribbean region was named. The Caribs were a warlike, cannibalistic people who originated in the western Caribbean and migrated from one island to another, seeking new conquests. Once established on a new island, they divided their time between military raids and fishing expeditions, which kept the group's men away from their home islands for long periods. When early explorers found only women and children on some of the islands they visited, they assumed they had encountered an all-female society. This mistaken impression was responsible for widespread legends about "Amazons"—woman warriors—who were said to populate the area.

The Caribs were skilled stone workers. Many examples of their stone tools and ceremonial objects have been uncovered in the Caribbean area, although none have been found in Barbados. Here, because the island had no workable stone, the Caribs made their implements from intricately carved seashells. Other Carib artifacts include tubes that were used to inhale the smoke of a burning plant during religious ceremonies. The Caribs called the plant *cohiba*, but Europeans named it for the tube through which it was inhaled: *tabaco*.

Always on the move, the Caribs abandoned Barbados before 1600. No other tribe succeeded them; thus, the European explorers found the island deserted. Spain arrived in the West Indies before any other European nations—Central America and the Caribbean soon came to be called "the Spanish Main." But Spain was not to hold exclusive power for long. By 1600, the British, the Dutch, the French, and the Danes had all established outposts in the Caribbean.

Settlement Begins

In 1625, John Powell, a British sea captain, landed on Barbados. The island was uninhabited and not yet claimed by any European nation. Powell decided that it was a good prospect for British settlement, and he planted a cross on its soil. Then, on a large tree, he carved the words, "James K. of E. and of this Island." Powell had claimed the land for his sovereign, James I, King of England.

When Powell returned to England, he told his employer, a wealthy nobleman and merchant named William Courteen, about the island. Sir William decided to organize a colonizing expedition to Barbados. He hired Captain Henry Powell, John's brother, to lead the expedition, which arrived in Barbados on February 27, 1627. After helping his 80-man crew set up camp and clear land for cultivation, Powell sailed to the northeastern coast of South America, where he hoped to acquire seeds and plants for his tiny colony.

Powell's mission was successful. He returned to Barbados with tobacco and cotton, along with 32 Arawak Indians who had agreed to show the settlers how to raise their new crops. (Following contemporary European practice, the colonists enslaved the Indians after accepting their help.) Soon after Henry Powell's return from South America, his brother John brought another 90 British settlers to the island.

The Barbadian colonists, who worked the land as Courteen's employees rather than as independent landowners, did well. Within a year, the Powell brothers brought a shipload of cotton and tobacco back to England, returning with additional settlers and more supplies. By 1629, the island's British population had risen to more than 1,600. Meanwhile, however, trouble was brewing back home.

After he succeeded King James, Charles I granted Barbados to one of his aristocratic friends, the Earl of Carlisle. In 1628, a party of Carlisle supporters landed in Barbados and built a settlement near the island's only natural harbor, which they named Carlisle Bay. Because the site featured an ancient bridge over a creek, probably built by Arawak Indians,

Oliver Cromwell forced a treaty known as the Barbados Charter upon the early English settlers.

they called it Bridgetown. The names of both bay and settlement—now the capital of Barbados—have survived to the present day.

Carlisle's men, speaking for their patron, announced that from then on, they were masters of the island. Not surprisingly, Courteen's followers, including acting governor John Powell, protested. The two groups disputed their claims for the next year, with the Carlisle group emerging victorious. But even then, political wrangling continued.

In 1642, civil war broke out in England, pitting the forces of Charles I against those of Puritan reformer Oliver Cromwell. Some of the king's supporters fled to Barbados, where they established large plantations. The war in England ended with the defeat of the Royalists and the execution of King Charles in 1649. The Barbadians, however, remained loyal to the crown, swearing allegiance to Charles II, the exiled son of the executed monarch. Cromwell responded to this act of colonial defiance by sending an armed fleet to Barbados.

The warships arrived in 1651, prepared to enforce Cromwell's authority. Instead of a battle, however, what followed was a peaceful agreement. The Barbadians agreed to accept Cromwell's rule; the Cromwellians agreed to allow the islanders to control their own financial affairs and local

When the English monarchy was restored, Charles II granted Barbados the right to a voice in its own government.

laws. This pact, known as the Barbados Charter, remained in effect until 1660, when royal rule was restored in England. Charles II granted Barbados the right to a continued voice in its own government, but he also imposed a tax of 4.5 percent on all its exports. This tax was a source of friction in later years.

From Tobacco to Sugar

Despite the political unrest in England, Barbadian planters had continued to thrive. Clearing more and more land, they produced increasingly profitable harvests. Cotton was a successful crop, but the island's mainstay was tobacco, which found eager buyers in Europe. In the late 1630s, however, Barbadian tobacco was suddenly faced with new and unbeatable competition from Virgina.

With much more land than Barbados, this British colony could grow more tobacco at lower cost. Europeans, furthermore, preferred the taste of Virginia's tobacco; unloaded at London's docks in 1638 were 1.1 million tons of tobacco from Barbados and 3.4 million tons from Virginia. By 1640, Virginia had taken over the world tobacco market, leaving Barbados on the edge of bankruptcy. Desperate, the island's planters searched for a new, more profitable crop. They found it in sugar, a discovery that would change life in Barbados forever.

Sugarcane, which had been brought to the New World by Spanish and Portuguese navigators in the early 1500s, had proved to be an immensely profitable crop. Particularly successful in its cultivation were Brazil's Dutch settlers, who ran their sugar plantations with black slaves from Africa.

Barbados had a substantial labor force, largely consisting of white indentured servants and English people who had been convicted of crimes and sentenced to service on the island. "Transportation"—forced resettlement to a colony—was a common punishment for English, Irish, and Scottish lawbreakers from the 17th to the 19th centuries. Because large numbers of such felons had been sent to Barbados, people transported to the West Indies were said to have been "barbadoed."

The island's white laborers, however, were still too few in number to work large-scale sugar plantations. Using the Brazilian system as a model, Barbadian planters began to import black slaves. In 1640, the island's population consisted of some 25,000 whites and a few hundred blacks. By 1685, the white population had dropped to 20,000, but blacks numbered about 46,000. Two hundred years later, blacks outnumbered whites by about 20 to 1. This vast alteration in Barbados's racial makeup was created by sugar.

Slave ships brought many African blacks to Barbados to work on the sugar plantations.

Sugar and Slavery

Sugarcane, which probably originated in India, has been cultivated for thousands of years. Introduced to Europeans in the 7th century, sugar was prized for both its taste and its supposed medicinal qualities, but it was a scarce luxury. Not until New World planters began to export it in the 16th century was it widely available in Europe.

The culture of sugarcane, a tall (up to 24 feet, or 7.3 meters), perennial grass that resembles bamboo, requires rich soil and a hot, damp climate. Before the development of modern agricultural methods, it also required the work of many hands. Barbados had the soil and the climate. What it lacked was labor. In the 1640s, its planters began to solve that problem by importing stupendous numbers of black slaves from Africa.

By the 1600s, slavery had been widespread in Africa for centuries. But the New World's demands for labor vastly intensified the trade in human beings. The Dutch and the Portuguese were the first European slave traders. They soon were joined by others, notably the British and the French.

Black Africans became the central element in an economic phenomenon known as the triangular trade. The triangle's first point was Europe, where manufactured goods were loaded onto trading vessels. The ships then went to Africa, where their captains exchanged the goods for slaves. The slaves were carried to the New World and traded for sugar, rum, and cotton; these were, in turn, carried across the Atlantic Ocean for sale in Europe. In later years, a similar triangular trade existed among the New England colonies, Africa, and the Caribbean.

Historians estimate that more than 10 million Africans were brought to the Caribbean during the days of the slave trade, making it history's largest forced migration. Jammed into reeking, dark, and filthy ships, as many as one-third of the captured Africans died before they completed the 10-week Atlantic crossing. Those who survived could look forward to laboring 18 hours a day in the canefields of the Caribbean.

The slaves worked even longer hours during harvest seasons. When sugarcane has finished its last growth, it must be cut immediately. Once cut, it must be processed within 48 hours, or the sugar in the plant's stalk will ferment, making it useless. The slaves who worked Barbados's vast plantations in the 17th century had no modern machinery to assist them. After they cut the cane with long, machete-like knives, they stripped it of leaves, chopped it into short lengths, and rushed it to the processing factory. There, they pushed it through iron rollers to extract the juice. The rollers were connected by gears to turnstiles, which the slaves pushed.

In later years, the turnstiles were pushed by horses and oxen; still later, they were powered by windmills. The cane factories are now run by electricity, but the island is dotted with the ruins of hundreds of stone-and-brick windmills.

After the slaves had extracted the cane's liquid, they boiled it in massive iron or copper kettles, using the squeezed-out stalks as fuel. Remaining in the kettles when most of the juice had boiled away were molasses and sugar crystals. Some of the molasses was used for making rum, the favorite alcoholic beverage of both the Old and the New Worlds. (Sometimes called "Barbados Kill-Devil," the island's rum was described by one 17th-century writer as "a hot, hellish, and terrible liquor.") The rest of the molasses was poured into huge barrels called puncheons. The slaves emptied the sugar crystals into clay pots to dry, then packed the dry sugar into hogsheads, or large casks.

Until the 20th century, windmills provided the power for the processing of sugarcane.

The final job facing the exhausted laborers was transportation. Loading the barrels of rum, puncheons of molasses, and hogsheads of sugar into two-wheeled, donkey-drawn carts, the slaves moved them to the seacoast. There, sailing ships awaited, ready to carry the products to consumers in Europe and North America.

Barbados's sugar plantations, as one historian put it, "rested on the shoulders of the African"—but they brought the African no reward. Not all slaves were viciously mistreated—although many were—but even those belonging to relatively humane planters were worked extremely hard, often punished for minor offenses, and deprived of human dignity. They lived in rough thatch huts outside their masters' compounds. Some communities even had regulations prohibiting any slave hut from having more than one room, one window, and one door.

The planters, however, lived like medieval kings. Often called "sugar barons," they built themselves huge, luxurious villas, some of which still stand on Barbados. These "great houses," which featured paneled libraries, sweeping mahogany staircases, and elaborate formal gardens, were stocked with Europe's finest linens, crystal, and wines. After visiting Barbados in 1700, one European wrote, "The houses are well built in the style of those in England with many glazed windows; they are magnificently furnished. In a word the whole place has an appearance of . . . wealth." Another visitor, commenting on his host's home, said, "It was a palace with which Aladdin himself might have been satisfied."

For half a century, Barbados held the undisputed title of sugar capital of the world. Although it was among Great Britain's smallest possessions, it supplied the parent country with more income—through private profits and government taxes on sugar—than any other colony.

Barbados continued to be a major sugar producer, but after the early 1700s, it lost its top position to Jamaica. This much larger Caribbean neighbor, which could produce more sugar at lower cost than Barbados, ruled the sugar market until the mid-1700s. Jamaica's place was taken by the French colony of Saint-Domingue (now Haiti), then by Puerto Rico and, later, by Cuba.

In the early 19th century, the Caribbean's "sugar islands" were rocked by a new and unlikely competitor: France. When Great Britain, which had long been at war with France, used its navy to seal off French seaports, all trade between the New World and France was halted. Deprived of sugar by the blockade, the French built experimental factories for the production of sugar from the silvery-white root plant commonly known as the

In the 17th century, "sugar barons" on Barbados built luxurious villas with the profits from their plantations.

sugar beet. The experiments were successful, and France was soon producing all the sugar it needed. After the British defeated the French in 1815, West Indian sugar reentered the market. By then, however, the sugar beet had created a permanent dent in Europe's demand for the West Indian product.

The End of Slavery

Many Europeans had been campaigning against slavery since the early 1700s. They scored their first victory in 1792, when Denmark declared the slave trade illegal. Great Britain and its colonies outlawed it in 1807, France and the Netherlands soon afterward. Last to ban the buying and selling of Africans was Spain, which abolished the trade in 1820. Despite the ban, the capture and importation of blacks continued for some years; according to some estimates, Cuba, for example, imported at least a half-million African slaves after the traffic had been prohibited.

After 1807, British activists began to fight for the complete abolition of slavery. Progress was slow, but they pushed through a few laws that improved the lives of the West Indian slaves. Now forbidden to use whips on field workers, planters were also required to free slaves who had enough money to buy their own liberty. These moves both heartened Barbados's slaves and made them increasingly impatient for freedom.

In 1816, slaves on several Barbadian plantations rose against their masters, setting fire to canefields and proclaiming their freedom. Poorly organized and virtually unarmed, the rebels were quickly defeated by government forces. Although no planters had been injured and only one soldier killed, the rebels were punished mercilessly. Hundreds were shot when they were captured, many more were executed after brief "trials," and others were flogged and deported in chains to distant islands.

After investigating the revolt, an Assembly committee announced that it had been the work of one person: Joseph Pitt Washington Francklyn, a free man "of color" (of mixed black and white ancestry). Ignoring the very real grievances of the rebels, the committee blamed their actions on

Francklyn, who had allegedly encouraged the revolt by talking to slaves about the emancipation movement. Condemned for his "crime," Francklyn was hanged. He is honored today as a national hero of Barbados.

The planters of the West Indies were horrified by the prospect of abolition, but it finally came to pass. Britain ended slavery at home and in its colonies on August 1, 1834. One by one, the other European colonial powers followed suit, but slowly. Not until 1886 were all West Indian slaves freed.

Emancipation had different effects on different islands. On many, the newly freed slaves refused to work for their former masters, migrating instead to unoccupied land and setting up their own small farms. On these islands, which included Jamaica and Trinidad, emancipation was followed by economic ruin: hundreds of once-flourishing plantations were neglected or abandoned entirely.

In Barbados, it was a different story. Here, almost every inch of land was under cultivation and legally owned. Without the means to leave the island, and without empty land on which to settle, Barbados's 83,176 former slaves had two choices: they could work for the planters or starve to death. They also had to work for whatever the planters were willing to pay them—which was, in most cases, very little. Nevertheless, they did receive some wages, and they were no longer subject to the plantation owners' every demand. They had no political rights, but in this, they were not alone. Only Barbados's few wealthy, white, male landowners and even fewer well-to-do "colored" men had such rights, and even these were limited.

The Colonial Government

At this time, Barbados was directly ruled by the British monarch. The king appointed the island's governor, who in turn appointed a legislative council. The island's day-to-day affairs were directed by the governor, the council, and the House of Assembly, whose members were elected. (Barbados's Assembly is the third oldest legislative body in the Western Hemisphere.

The first and second are those of Bermuda and the state of Virginia.) According to law, any adult male landowner who was a member of the Church of England was entitled to vote and to run for election to the Assembly. In practice, however, few nonwhites voted, and none was ever nominated for the legislature.

One man, Samuel Jackman Prescod, decided to change this state of affairs. Born to a free black mother and a white father in 1806, Prescod spent his life working toward equality for all Barbadians. Largely as a result of his determined efforts, free colored (mixed-race) men were granted the right to vote in 1831. Prescod demanded justice for all races. "Mere complexion," he wrote, "has nothing to do with the case." Continuing his fight for the underprivileged, Prescod took over a radical Bridgetown newspaper, the *Liberal*. Prescod's literary and political skills soon earned the widespread respect of both whites and blacks, and in 1843, he was nominated for a seat in the Assembly.

After an election campaign that one observer called "the hottest ever known in Barbados," Prescod was elected, thus becoming the first non-white ever to hold office on the island. He served as a legislator for 20 years and wrote many laws that improved the lives of his fellow citizens. Today, Prescod is honored as a national hero. His likeness appears on Barbadian currency and the island's prestigious polytechnic school bears his name.

In the 19th century, the bulk of Barbados's lower class, a mixture of black former slaves and white descendants of indentured servants, lived in clusters of wooden buildings called "chattel houses." Chattel is an old legal term for any moveable article of property, which is exactly what these dwellings were. They were built from prefabricated kits—probably the first in history—that planters ordered from North America. Often owned by their inhabitants, they stood on ground rented from plantation owners, who were unwilling to sell any of their land. To this day, many Barbadians live in chattel houses, which, like their predecessors, occupy plots rented from large landowners.

The Nelson Monument in Bridgetown's Trafalgar Square honors the British admiral who defeated Napoleon's fleet.

Another souvenir of the 19th century is the Nelson monument in Bridgetown's Trafalgar Square. Dedicated in 1813, this landmark honors Horatio Nelson, the British admiral who defeated Napoleon at the Battle of Trafalgar, off the coast of Spain, in 1805. Nelson's visit to Bridgetown just before his death made him a special hero to Barbadians. London, England, has its own Trafalgar Square and its own monument to Nelson, but Barbadians have long noted with pride that their tribute to Nelson dates from before the London memorial.

Although Barbados had long ceased to be the world's leading producer of sugar, its sugar industry continued to be profitable through much of the 19th century. In the 1890s, however, the island's economy was hit by a series of disasters. First came a worldwide drop in sugar prices, then a drought, then an invasion of cane-destroying insects called moth borers. The island's difficulties were intensified by the major hurricane of 1898, which took hundreds of lives and destroyed thousands of homes.

The financial distress created by these calamities was partly offset by the construction of the Panama Canal. Between 1906 and 1913, a wave of Barbadian men emigrated to Panama, joining the international workforce whose labors would, in 1913, produce a waterway connecting the Atlantic and Pacific oceans. Money sent home by Barbadian canal workers enabled thousands of previously landless families to buy small farms. Barbados's economy also received a boost from the increased demand for West Indian sugar created by World War I (1914–1918).

Like much of the rest of the world, Barbados was hit hard by the Great Depression of the 1930s, which produced widespread unemployment, strikes, hunger marches, and riots. An investigation of the island's troubles led to public works programs and the establishment of workmen's compensation, unemployment insurance, and a minimum wage. Growing from these economic reforms was political change: In 1944, women received the right to vote and to run for the Assembly; in 1951, all income and property qualifications for voters were removed; in 1963, the vote was extended to all Barbadians over the age of 18.

About 95 percent of the Barbadian population is of black ancestry.

The People of Barbados

The word *Barbadian* is usually pronounced "bar-BAY-dee-un." But to the British, who owned and occupied Barbados for more than three centuries, and whose style of speech is entirely their own, the word is "bar-BAY-jun." Based on this pronunciation is the term "Bajan," a nickname for native-born islanders. "Bim," its origin unknown, is another British-coined nickname for a Barbadian, and "Bimshire" refers to the nation.

About 95 percent of Barbados's people are of black African ancestry. Most of them are descended from people who have lived on the island for centuries. Three percent of the islanders are white; the rest are Asians and people of mixed racial backgrounds. The island's official language is English, but most of its residents also speak a local dialect that includes words of African and 18th-century English as well as modern English. *Nyam* (eat) and *duppy* (ghost), for example, are from Africa, while "Mistress" for "Mrs." echoes the England of centuries past.

Barbados gained its independence from Britain in 1966. Although it retains strong echoes of the nation that ruled it since the 17th century, the island has an atmosphere that is distinctly its own, a blend of staunchly British traditions and uniquely Barbadian patterns. The island's residents are, for example, fond of such British customs as afternoon tea, complete with tiny cucumber sandwiches, buttered scones (biscuits), and marmalade (preserves made with bitter oranges). But they also relish their own culinary specialties, which include coconut soup, curried goat, turtle steak, and doved peas (green peas browned in oil).

Inherited from the British is the Barbadians' admiration for military pageantry. The maneuvers of crisply uniformed marching bands and well-trained mounted guards, both souvenirs of the British presence, remain popular in Bridgetown, the nation's capital. Distinctly un-British, however, is the islanders' enthusiasm for steel bands, whose ever-present, rhythmic music is played on carefully tuned oil drums. Barbadians share the British love of polo matches and horse races. And the game of cricket, another British import, is often called Barbados's "national passion."

Barbados's population, like that of most countries, includes a handful of very wealthy people, a small number of poor people, and a large majority of middle-class, working families. The income, interests, and life-styles of these groups may differ sharply, but their taste for cricket forms a common bond. Almost everyone in Barbados seems to enjoy either watching or playing the game.

A full cricket team consists of 11 players, but any two people with a bat and a ball can practice. "It is almost impossible to travel through any district in daylight hours," observes former Bridgetown mayor Louis Lynch, "without coming upon a group of youngsters playing the game with improvised equipment." Bridgetown businessmen on their way to work often carry a briefcase in one hand, a cricket bat in the other.

Cricket matches between villages are guaranteed large crowds of spectators, and people of all classes and races flock to Garrison Savannah, just outside Bridgetown, to see matches between Barbados and visiting teams from overseas. For its size and population, Barbados has probably produced more world-famous cricketers than any nation in the world. Among its most celebrated stars are the "Three Ws," Frank Worrell, C. L. Walcott, and Everton Weekes. Knighted for his accomplishments by Britain's Queen Elizabeth II, Worrell is pictured on the Barbadian $5 bill. "Cricket in Barbados," jokes Louis Lynch, "is not a game but a religion."

(continued on page 57)

SCENES OF
BARBADOS

►
Windmills, once used in the sugarcane industry, still dot the island.

◄ *The climate and lush tropical scenery draw tourists from all over the world.*

▼
Cannons placed in fortified positions along the coast guarded Barbados in more turbulent times.

▲ *Brightly painted warehouses line the harbor of Bridgetown.*

▼ *Barbadian women often wear colorful clothing with vibrant prints.*

▼ *Barbados's educational system has produced a population with almost universal literacy.*

◄ *Sugar remains one of Barbados's major exports.*

▼ *Cricket is the national pastime in Barbados.*

▲ *Some sections of Barbados, such as these rolling hills, bear a resemblance to the English countryside.*

► *Tourism is a major source of revenue for the Barbadian economy.*

◄ *In Bridgetown, tropical vegetation and English architecture mingle.*

►
Codrington College is the oldest degree-granting institution in the English-speaking Caribbean.

▼ *Fishing, as both sport and industry, is an increasingly important feature of the Barbadian economy.*

(continued from page 48)

On a more serious note, religion plays an important role in Barbados. Only 5 percent of the nation's people identify themselves as "nonreligious." Most of the population (about 80 percent) is Protestant; more than half of this group is affiliated with the Church of England. Other Protestant denominations include Methodist, Pentecostal, and Seventh-day Adventist. Some 7 percent of the islanders are Roman Catholic. The Church of England, or Anglican Church, was once Barbados's only legal religion, but its embrace of blacks was sometimes sharply questioned.

In 1827, Anglican clergyman W. M. Harte was accused of distributing communion to slaves. Such "disgraceful conduct," said his white congregation, would "alienate their slaves from a sense of their duty" and interfere with their "obedience to their masters and the policy of the island." Harte stood trial three times. He was found guilty and ordered to pay a fine, but he was pardoned after he appealed his sentence to George IV of England. The royal pardon, wrote one chronicler, provided "great gratification" to "the numerous admirers of the Christian virtues of Mr. Harte." White ministers of other denominations, notably the Quakers and Methodists, also worked to improve the life of Barbados's slaves and, eventually, to free them. Today, most of the island's pastors, like their congregations, are black.

Birth of Native Culture

Barbados's blacks, like other enslaved peoples throughout history, had been taught to think of their masters as superior beings. They had been separated from their hereditary culture and denied basic education and legal rights for centuries. Not surprisingly, then, they emerged from slavery with little faith in their own abilities. For many years after emancipation, black Barbadians modeled themselves and their life-styles on British examples. They did this so effectively that Barbados was often called "Little England."

As the years passed, however, Barbadians came to take pride in their own culture and to develop their own creative abilities. Today, the islanders maintain only those British customs they consider important in themselves. The nation, in short, has gained the confidence to be itself.

Samuel Jackman Prescod, the first Barbadian of "color" to sit in the House of Assembly, was also among the first nonwhite Barbadians to make a name for himself in journalism. Editor of the *Liberal,* he proved to blacks and whites alike that skin shade had little to do with literary skill. Barbados produced a handful of writers in succeeding years, but they worked in isolation, without the backing of an artistic community or serious public interest. It was not until the 1930s, when Barbadian nationalism began to exert its influence, that the island's art movement began to take shape.

The maneuvers of crisply uniformed marching bands remain a popular spectacle in Bridgetown.

Gradually, as "Bajans" found their voices, more and more distinctively Barbadian poetry and fiction appeared. In 1942, Frank A. Collymore, a black writer and teacher, and E. L. (Jimmy) Cozier, a white journalist, started a magazine called *Bim*. Designed as a showcase for native literary talent, *Bim* introduced the work of a number of writers, including George Lamming. Among Lamming's celebrated novels are *In the Castle of My Skin* and *Season of Adventure*.

After author and meteorologist John Wickham became its editor in the 1970s, *Bim* published the work of such internationally respected novelists as Andrew Salkey (*The Late Emancipation of Jerry Stover*), Earl Lovelace (*The Schoolmaster*), Michael Anthony (*The Year in San*

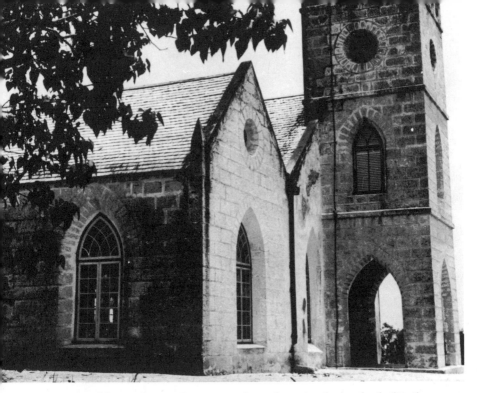

Most of the population is Protestant and attends services in churches built in the Anglican style.

Fernando), and Wilson Harris (*Tumatumari*), as well as works by such poets as Anthony La Rose (*Foundations*) and L. Edward Brathwaite (*Rights of Passage*).

Barbados's writers have a rich store of local facts and legends on which to draw. One often retold story concerns the cemetery at Christ Church, a few miles from Bridgetown. Here—still standing—is a stone burial vault built in 1742. The first coffin was placed in the vault, which is partly above and partly below ground level, in 1807.

Over the next 13 years, seven new coffins were brought to the sealed vault. Each time it was opened, shocked mourners saw the same eerie sight: all the coffins, each made of lead and weighing about 500 pounds, were strewn about, some propped against the walls, others standing on their heads.

Local residents became increasingly uneasy about the strange events at Christ Church cemetery, and in 1820, the island's governor, Lord Combermere, decided to settle the mystery. After proving that the vault had no underground passageways, he ordered it locked and completely coated with cement. To demonstrate the absence of ghosts, he returned soon afterward, accompanied by a crowd of witnesses and a team of stonemasons. They found the cement undisturbed, the lock unbroken.

The masons broke the vault open—and stared in horror. Scattered about, even more violently than before, were seven broken coffins, from one of which poked a skeletal arm. At this point, Combermere gave up his efforts to disprove the supernatural. He ordered the dead removed and buried elsewhere, leaving the vault empty, as it remains today. A number of researchers, including a team from the London Science Museum, have

Barbados's writers draw on the rich store of local facts and legends. One of the most famous legends concerns the mysterious events in a local cemetery.

investigated the "coffin mystery," but no one has ever solved it. None of the witnesses to the ghoulish doings at the cemetery are, of course, available for questioning today. Were the events exaggerated? Quite possibly, but the story remains a fascinating sample of island lore.

In recent years, creative Barbadians have shown increasing interest in portraying their distinctive lifestyles and the natural beauty of their surroundings. Many of the island's dancers, musicians, painters, and sculptors, along with its novelists and poets, now concentrate on Barbadian themes. These artists are showcased and encouraged by such groups as the Barbados Dance Theater Company, the Arts Council, the Country Theater Workshop, and the Barbados Writers' Guild.

The most celebrated of Barbados's artisans are its potters, who fashion a great variety of objects.

Barbados is home to a flourishing community of skilled artisans. The nation's wood carvers are known for their sensitive renditions of local birds and flying fish. Other folk artists weave native grasses into intricately patterned mats and wall hangings; still others create mosaiclike scenes from the tiny seashells found in profusion on the island's beaches.

Perhaps most celebrated of Barbados's artisans are its potters, who use clay from the Scotland District's Chalky Mount to fashion a wide variety of pitchers, jugs, and other ornamental and useful objects. Patterns from tools and pottery fragments, recently unearthed at prehistoric Barbadian campsites, have provided an exciting new theme for the island's potters.

The financial administration of Barbados is centered in the Treasury Building in Bridgetown.

Government and Economy

As a member of the Commonwealth of Nations (formerly called the British Commonwealth), Barbados is technically ruled by the British monarch. That monarch (currently Elizabeth II) appoints a head of state known as the governor-general. These officials, however, hold symbolic, rather than actual, power. The governor-general, who has little legal authority, is really selected by the prime minister, the nation's chief executive.

Barbados's government consists of three branches: legislative, executive, and judicial. The legislature, or law-making branch, consists of two sections, the 27-member House of Assembly and the 21-member Senate. Assembly members are elected by voters in each of the island's 27 constituencies, or districts. (Since 1963, all Barbadian men and women over the age of 18 are eligible to vote.) The Senate comprises 19 members of the majority party, selected by the prime minister, and 2 members of the opposition, or minority party in the Assembly. All members of the legislature serve five-year terms.

The nation's executive branch is composed of the prime minister, who is the leader of the majority party in the Assembly, and the cabinet. Cabinet ministers, appointed by the prime minister, are drawn from Assembly and Senate members of the majority party. Each minister is responsible for one or more government departments, such as education or finance.

The third section of Barbados's government, the judiciary, is headed by the chief justice of the Supreme Court. Like the nation's senators, the chief justice is appointed by the governor-general on the recommendation of the prime minister. Under the chief justice are three puisne (pronounced pyoo-nee), or associate, judges, who hear cases and serve as a court of appeal. Minor criminal and civil cases are tried by district magistrates.

Barbados's ministerial form of government began in 1954, when Sir Grantley Adams, a black Barbadian lawyer and a graduate of Britain's Oxford University, became premier. Adams, a longtime crusader for Barbadian independence and the founder of the Barbados Labor Party (BLP), served as premier until 1958. After his death in 1971, the island's principal airport was named in his honor—Grantley Adams International.

In 1961, the BLP lost the national election to the island's other major political organization, the Democratic Labor Party (DLP). The DLP is closely allied to Barbados's principal labor group, the Barbados Workers' Union. The BLP and the DLP have similar names and goals.

Both parties favor moderate, democratic policies. Like the British Labor Party, both have socialist leanings, believing that it is the government's responsibility to provide the public with free education from grade school through college, free health care, guaranteed minimum wages, affordable housing, unemployment and disability insurance, and retirement income. Although the BLP and the DLP agree on most goals, they disagree on the most effective means of achieving them.

Independence

At midnight on November 30, 1966, Barbados ended its 340-year history as a British colony. It became an independent nation within the Commonwealth of Nations. Errol Barrow, who had been its premier since 1961, was the island's first prime minister. He was the leader of the DLP.

The DLP held power from 1961 until 1976. When the BLP won the 1976 election, J.M.G.M. (Tom) Adams, Grantley Adams's son, became prime minister. The younger Adams was known for his conservative approach to politics; for example, he strongly backed the 1983 U.S.-led invasion of the Caribbean island of Grenada. He died in 1985. The election of 1986 returned the DLP to power under Prime Minister Errol Barrow. Barrow died the following year, and was succeeded as prime minister by the new leader of the DLP, Erskine Sandiford.

Barbados's women acquired the right to vote in 1944, 16 years after their British counterparts. Since that time, women have been appointed to the Senate and have served as ministers, but few have been elected to the Assembly. By the late 1980s, no woman had occupied the office of prime minister, leader of the opposition, or governor-general.

Barbados maintains ties to Great Britain by its membership in the Commonwealth of Nations, but relations with its former ruler are minimal. As a member of the Commonwealth, it enjoys a preferential status in the European Economic Community, or Common Market. This means that it can sell its products in Western Europe without paying stiff customs, or taxes. A second link between Barbados and Britain is judicial: a citizen who wishes to appeal a Barbadian court decision may take his or her case to Britain's House of Lords, the upper house of Parliament.

Barbados's governmental structure is based on that of Great Britain, but unlike the parent country, Barbados has a written constitution. (Great Britain's laws are based not on a formal constitution, but on the Magna Carta, a document signed in the year 1215.) Adopted at independence, Barbados's Constitution has much in common with the U.S. Constitution and its Bill of Rights. Both charters guarantee such basic rights as freedom of the press and of religion, and both provide for an independent judicial system and universal suffrage (the right of every adult citizen to vote).

Natural Resources and Revenue

Barbados's greatest natural resource is its climate. The island's temperatures, combined with its usually sunny skies, attract some 500,000 tourists each year—almost twice Barbados's population. The island's comfortable

weather allows the fishing industry to operate all year; it also benefits farmers, who can grow year-round crops of sugarcane, fruits, and vegetables.

The island has a plentiful supply of limestone and sandstone, which are used in manufacturing cement, but it lacks such basic industrial natural resources as coal, iron, and timber. Recently discovered natural gas

*The island's consistently warm weather
is ideal for the sugarcane industry.*

and offshore oil, however, now provide about half the nation's energy
needs.

Gross national product (GNP) is the total value of all the goods and
services produced by a country during one year. In 1986, Barbados's GNP
equalled $1.3 billion (U.S. dollars). The average annual Barbadian income
equalled U.S. $4,700. One Barbados dollar equals about 50 cents in U.S.

currency, but it buys as much in Barbados as one U.S. dollar buys in the United States. A Barbadian earning U.S. $4,700 per year would thus have the buying power of a U.S. resident who earned $9,400.

Barbadians' income, of course, varies; some people earn more than the national average; some earn less. Nevertheless, the nation has one of the Caribbean area's highest standards of living. On a per-person basis, it is among the world's most prosperous nations.

Although tourism and agriculture are the most visible sources of income in Barbados, they account for slightly less than 20 percent of the

island's GNP. Once the mainstay of the island's economy, the sugar industry is in a slump, and produced only about 15 percent of the island's export income in 1986. In recent years, the cost of producing sugar has been higher than the price received for it. The European Common Market guarantees the price that Barbados sugar exporters will be paid for their product. In 1986, this guarantee was U.S. 25 cents per pound. It cost Barbados's planters, however, 28 cents per pound to produce the sugar. Unless the world's demand for sugar increases sharply, the industry's decline is expected to continue.

The manufacture and export of rum is a traditional and profitable enterprise.

Nearly half of Barbados's income is derived from three sources: manufacturing, wholesale and retail sales, and business services. Many of the corporations that operate on the island are foreign-owned. Barbados has a number of assets that attract overseas-based companies (also known as TNCs, or transnational corporations). Among them is the island's stable government. Not since the depression-sparked riots of the 1930s has Barbados seen serious local unrest and, unlike several of its neighbors, it has never had a revolution. Its currency is also stable, which means that it retains approximately the same international value from one year to the next. U.S. and British business operators are further drawn to Barbados because its native language is English and because its literacy rate is one of the highest in the world.

Transnational corporations provide jobs and other revenue; Barbados's government therefore encourages them to locate on the island. Among the incentives offered to the TNCs are favorable tax rules and new, government-built industrial parks. To advertise the nation's good points as a manufacturing location, Barbadian development officials distribute a film called *Barbados, the Profitable Paradise.* The boosters' slogan is "You can judge an island by the companies it keeps."

Manufacturers of clothing and electronic equipment have been especially responsive to Barbados's possibilities. Typically, these companies bring premanufactured components into Barbados for assembly into finished products. The goods are then packaged for export to world markets. Operations of this type have been successful, but their future, some trade analysts believe, is uncertain, largely because of Barbados's minimum-wage law. Taiwan, China, South Korea, and other countries with lower labor costs may pose a threat to Barbados's product-assembly factories. Their loss would be a sharp blow to the economy of the island, which has an unemployment rate of approximately 18 percent.

Not surprisingly, young, college-educated Barbadians are reluctant to work on sugar plantations or dairy farms. Many would prefer jobs in the island's manufacturing sector or in the tourist industry, but there are not enough jobs in these areas to absorb them. In past years, ambitious Barbadians often emigrated to the United States, Canada, and Great Britain. There, they found jobs to match their qualifications, sending part of their earnings back to their families in Barbados. As unemployment has increased in recent years, however, new immigration regulations have made it more difficult for outsiders, including Barbadians, to enter these countries.

Like many nations, Barbados spends more than it earns. Contributing to this problem is the island's heavy importation of food. Although Barbados cultivates more of its land (about 60 percent) than any other Caribbean nation, it has always consumed more food than it produces. Hoping to reduce costly food imports, government officials have mounted a vigorous effort to expand and diversify the nation's agricultural output. This campaign has been particularly effective among dairy and poultry farmers, who have enlarged and modernized their operations. The government also offers financial support to the fishing industry.

Barbados is not faced with the expense of equipping and paying a large military force. Aware that it could never resist an attack by a large nation, it fields only a tiny army, the 150-person Barbados Defense Force. This group provides rescue services for victims of accidents at sea, helps to keep order during such natural disasters as hurricanes, and assists drug-enforcement officials in combating the production and importation of illegal drugs. Barbados also maintains a 1,000-person national police force. Its male and female officers, who wear colorful red, black, and gray uniforms, are unarmed.

Barbados's educational system has achieved the highest literacy rate in the West Indies.

Health and Education

Europeans faced many threats in the New World, but the most dangerous was disease. Epidemics wiped out many more settlers than all other causes of death, including warfare. Malaria and yellow fever, spread by mosquitoes that thrived in the hot, humid climate, were particularly deadly.

Barbados was largely spared from these afflictions. The island's terrain, well drained and thoroughly cleared by early settlers, harbored few pools of stagnant water, and trade winds carried off much of the air's moisture. These conditions suppressed the mosquito population, thereby keeping the death rate from malaria and yellow fever low.

Although it escaped many of the murderous plagues that swept its neighbors, Barbados did experience one major epidemic. Aboard a ship that arrived in Bridgetown in 1854 were several seamen afflicted with cholera, a highly contagious and usually fatal disease. In the mid-19th century, few people in the West Indies—or in Europe—understood the importance of sanitation in preventing disease. Even when the cholera brought by the sailors began to spread through Bridgetown, no steps were taken to keep sewage from contaminating drinking water. In a very short time, the disease had flashed through the island, killing some 20,000 Barbadians.

Meanwhile, British doctors were becoming aware that epidemics were often started by infected patients and spread by contaminated water. In

1869, the British government passed laws calling for the protection of public water supplies and the quarantining (keeping apart) of people suffering from contagious diseases. Soon adopted in Barbados and other British Caribbean islands, these measures sharply reduced deaths by disease. By 1886, Barbados had constructed a centralized system that supplied pure water to all parts of the island.

Public health care, which began with district medical officers in the late 1800s, has increased in scope since Barbados became independent in 1966. The Barbadian government owns and operates Queen Elizabeth Hospital, an 800-bed facility that serves as a teaching hospital for the medical school of the University of the West Indies. Also government-operated is the modern Psychiatric Hospital in the parish of St. Michael. Scattered around the island are nursing homes designed to care for chronic invalids and the elderly.

Under construction in 1988 were a series of clinics, which are expected to provide extensive outpatient medical and family-planning services. Barbados's public schools deliver free immunization services and dental and ophthalmic (eye) care to the island's children. A program offering free prescription drugs for the poor and the elderly began operating in the mid-1980s.

Barbados's vital statistics (figures that concern human life and the conditions that affect it) are impressive. Life expectancy is high: men born between 1980 and 1985 could expect to reach the age of 67.6 years, women the age of 72.5 years. (By comparison, the average life expectancy in the United States for the same period was 74.7 years; for the Caribbean nation of Jamaica, 65 years; for the African republic of Liberia, 54 years.)

The number of Barbadian babies who die at birth (the infant mortality rate) has been dropping steadily; for 1985, the figure was 25.1 deaths per thousand births. Also in 1985, Barbados's birthrate (the number of babies born for each 1,000 people on the island) was 16.8, compared to a world average of 29. Its death rate per thousand people was 8.4, compared to a world average of 11.

Another noteworthy statistic is the high rate (about 75 percent) of Barbadian children born to unmarried parents. Most of the island's women have been self-supporting for centuries; for this reason, perhaps, few have felt the need to marry for financial security. In many countries, high rates of birth to unmarried women are associated with high rates of infant mortality. This is not the case in Barbados.

Barbados is untroubled by major air-pollution problems. The island has very little heavy industry, and the trade winds quickly sweep vehicle exhaust fumes out to sea. Pollution does, however, pose a potential problem to the sea around Barbados. Most household "gray water"—water used for bathing and washing—runs into the ocean. In recent decades, detergents in this runoff have begun to change the composition of the offshore water. Construction of a new waste-treatment system, which will handle both gray water and sewage, began in 1981. Officals expect it to be completed before offshore marine life is seriously damaged.

Like the United States and many other countries, Barbados is alarmed by the rising use of illegal drugs. The Barbados Defense force has stepped up both its efforts to intercept drug shipments arriving by sea and its search-and-destroy attacks on the island's marijuana crops. Customs inspections for incoming travelers, too, have been tightened.

Education

All of Barbados's educational institutions, public and private, nursery school through college, operate under the supervision of the Ministry of Education. The ministry defines its goal: to teach each Barbadian "to live harmoniously in his (or her) environment and to make a useful contribution to the economic society."

Barbados's educational system has produced one of the world's most literate populations: almost every adult in the nation can read and write. In the 1986–87 school year, 50,487 pupils attended Barbadian public schools below college level. Another 7,028 children were enrolled in private schools, and 5,892 students attended colleges and technical schools.

Education in Barbados has a long history. The first "charity," or free, public school was established in 1686 by a group of planters. In the years that followed, other wealthy Barbadians established schools; plantation owner Christopher Codrington endowed a college to train missionaries in 1710. Now the oldest degree-granting institution in the English-speaking Caribbean, Codrington College continues to educate future members of the clergy from all over the West Indies and beyond.

Although clergymen from several Protestant faiths made attempts to educate Barbados's slaves, their efforts were usually frustrated by slave-

In the 1986–1987 school year, more than 50,000 pupils attended Barbardian public schools below college level.

owners. Universal public education in Barbados got its real start between 1825 and 1842. During this period, the Anglican bishop of Barbados, William Hart Coleridge, built more than 200 schools across the nation. When slavery was abolished in 1834, Coleridge and his associates opened schools for the former slaves and their children.

By the beginning of the 20th century, the government was largely supporting the island's schools, but most were still operated by the Anglican church and other denominations. An era of educational change began in 1943, when the Department (later called Ministry) of Education was

established. At this point, teachers became civil servants (government employees) and the educational structure was reorganized. The schools were divided into three groups: infant, junior, and senior. Teaching methods were overhauled and students were assigned to classes on the basis of intelligence-test results. In 1976, the compulsory-attendance age was raised from 14 to 16.

Today, many Barbadian children start their educations at the age of three, when they enter nursery school. Their formal schooling begins when they are five. After six years in primary school, the children take examinations. Those with the best scores are admitted to one of the island's secondary schools (high schools), where courses include such subjects as algebra, geometry, history, English, and Spanish. Students with lower test grades are assigned to one of the senior schools, which offer remedial academic work and vocational courses.

Barbados also operates four schools for students with special needs. The School for the Deaf and the Blind, which opened in 1959, now enrolls about 80 handicapped children whose ages range from 3 to 18. Attending the School for the Mentally Retarded are about 60 students from 11 to 24 years of age. Two Government Industrial Schools, one for boys and one for girls, are operated for youngsters referred by the Juvenile Court.

The government operates a school for the mentally retarded, attended by about 60 students ranging in age from 11 to 24 years.

Like their British counterparts, Barbados's schools require students to take an examination before passing from one school level to another. The examination taken for entrance to secondary school is called a "screening test." (Students, however, have been known to refer to it as "the screaming test.") After finishing secondary school, students must pass the CXC, an examination designed by the Caribbean Examination Council, before they can be considered for college entrance.

Students admitted to the Barbados branch of the University of the West Indies pay no tuition. In 1987–1987, 1,728 students were enrolled at the university. Students who are not accepted at the university have several alternatives. These include two-year programs at Erdiston Training College (for teachers), Barbados Community College (for commercial and technical training), and Samuel Jackman Prescod Polytechnic (for training in trades and crafts). In addition to serving fulltime students, these institutions offer a variety of evening courses and part-time programs for adults.

Extracurricular activities available to Barbados's students at all levels include clubs, hobby groups, and almost every sport not requiring ice and snow. In addition to school-related activities, young people participate in church-affiliated groups, Boy Scouts, Girl Guides (the British version of Girl Scouts), the YWCA/YMCA, 4-H chapters, and clubs sponsored by labor unions and the two major political parties.

Grantley Adams International Airport, the largest in the West Indies, is a full-service facility.

Transportation and Communication

Branching out from Bridgetown are about 1,000 miles of roads, most of them narrow but paved with concrete or asphalt. Sharing these roads—where drivers keep to the left, British-style—are pedestrians, cars, trucks, buses, bicycles, goats, and donkey carts. Because of congestion and the steep hills and blind curves, traffic rarely exceeds 30 miles per hour.

Driving around Barbados offers unusual prospects for visitors. As travel writer Margaret Zellers has noted, "Barbados wears a blanket of sugarcane from December until cane-cutting season in late May or June. When the cane is tall, you can drive across the midsection of the island without being able to see anything but a wall of green fronds, reminiscent—for those who have driven in England—of the narrow, hedgerow-lined roads in the southwest."

Roadside attractions include St. Ann's Fort, built on the outskirts of Bridgetown in 1703, and several "Great Houses" that date back to the planters of the 1600s. Drivers crossing the center of the island will encounter Welchman's Hall Gully, a plantation maintained by the Barbados National Trust. The Gully presents samples of almost every flower, shrub, and tree native to the area. One of the island's main roads leads directly from Bridgetown to the dramatic Bathsheba Coast, where rugged cliffs overlook thunderous, surf-pounded Atlantic Ocean beaches.

One of the island's main roads leads directly from Bridgetown to the Dramatic Bathsheba coast.

Barbados has no railroads; all freight is transported by truck. The Barbadian government operates an efficient bus system, which carries passengers to all points of the island. A visitor, however, is more likely to use one of the many taxis that cluster around the airport and downtown Bridgetown. Cabdrivers and private owners usually select small Japanese models, best suited for Barbados's narrow city streets and winding country roads. Registered on the island are 31,000 automobiles and 5,500 trucks and buses.

Barbados's most heavily traveled road is Highway 1, which runs the length of the island along its west coast. A new, limited-access superhighway, under construction in the late 1980s, is expected to decrease traffic on the coastal road and speed up travel to the airport.

Because of its small size, Barbados has no internal air service. Grantley Adams International Airport, however, is a full-service facility, connecting the island with the United States, Canada, South America, and Europe, as well as the rest of the Caribbean. Many international travelers consider Adams International the West Indies' finest air terminal.

Barbados is linked to the rest of the world not only by air service, but by telephone, telegraph, radio, and television. Telegraph service, in fact, reached the island in 1872, and "cable radio" has been available for almost 50 years. Cable radios, which are directly connected by telephone lines to radio station VOB-790 (the Voice of Barbados), are a feature in almost every home on the island.

Most households also contain telephones, radios, and television sets. Direct-dialing telephone communication is made possible by a huge satellite receiver and transmitter situated on the east coast. The satellite also brings in television shows from the United States and Canada, which supply the bulk of the island's programs. A major exception is sports coverage; games of cricket, Barbados's national obsession, are broadcast live and at full length.

Barbados's two major newspapers, the *Advocate* and the *Nation*, provide thorough national and international news coverage. Their outspoken discussion and criticism of the government offer strong evidence of Barbados's Constitution-guaranteed freedom of the press. Also lively reading is the *Bajan*, an illustrated monthly newsmagazine. Two other publications, the *Barbados Tourist News* and *The Visitor*, list activities and sightseeing opportunities for the island's thousands of vacationers.

The postal system of Barbados began in 1663 as part of the British mail service. In 1858, the island took over its own postal service, opening offices in Bridgetown and in each of the 10 outlying parishes. Since then, five more district post offices have been established. Mail is delivered to Bridgetown residents twice each day from the large modern central post office on the city's waterfront. Other areas receive one mail delivery per day. Admired by collectors all over the world, the nation's postage stamps have pictures of colorful native flowers, birds, and marine life, as well as historical events.

Barbados is a beautiful, tranquil island with a long tradition of democratic government.

Barbados: An Overview

A British colony for more than 300 years, Barbados has been independent since 1966. Today, the West Indian island-nation is a model of nonviolent transition from minority-ruled colony to majority-ruled democracy.

Most of Barbados's citizens are black, the descendants of Africans brought to the New World as sugar-plantation slaves. Emancipated in 1834, the island's blacks gradually—and peacefully—acquired the right to own land, to vote, to run for public office, and finally, to take control of their own nation. Although most government officials are black, the rights of the nation's white minority are scrupulously respected.

Barbados is one of the world's most densely populated countries. It is also one of its most literate. Relatively few Barbadians are truly wealthy, but their per-person income is among the highest in the world. Barbadians also have an impressively high life expectancy.

Once almost wholly dependent on sugar, Barbados's economy has become diversified, with manufacturing and tourism among its most important elements. Some 500,000 tourists—twice the number of local residents—visit the island each year. They are attracted by its uniformly warm temperatures, clear skies, white beaches, and sparkling blue water.

Like many nations, Barbados is burdened by both a trade imbalance (it imports more than it exports) and a fairly high (18 percent) unemploy-

Two Barbadians converse in a quiet moment on the docks of Bridgetown.

ment rate. To correct its trade deficit, provide more revenue, and increase job opportunities, the government is making a vigorous effort to attract foreign investments and to stimulate domestic industry and agriculture.

Although it is not without problems, Barbados can take justified pride in its many assets and achievements. It is a beautiful, tranquil island with a long tradition of democratic government. Its people are well educated, healthy, and generally prosperous. On the international scene, it has worked to increase aid to developing countries and to end terrorism. Avoiding involvement in conflicts between the great powers, Barbados maintains friendly relations with all the world's nations.

Like other West Indian musicians, Barbadians are adept with drum and pipe.

◄GLOSSARY►

Bajan A slang form of the name Barbadian, used to refer to native-born islanders.

Bim A nickname for Barbadians. It originated with the British, but its meaning is unknown.

Bimshire A British nickname for Barbados.

Chattel houses Prefabricated houses that were built from kits. Called chattels because they were a form of moveable property, the houses were owned by the people who lived in them but stood on land rented from the landowners. People could move the houses from one rented plot to another. Chattel houses are still used in Barbados.

Cohiba Carib Indian for "tobacco." The Caribs used tobacco smoke in religious ceremonies.

Indentured servants Men and women who agreed to work without pay for a period of from three to seven years, in return for transportation to the New World.

Mongoose A small, weasel- or ferret-like carnivorous mammal native to India. It was imported to Barbados to hunt and kill rats and now flourishes on the island.

Puisne judges Associate judges under the Barbadian judicial system. Three puisne judges serve under the chief justice; they hear cases and form an appeals court.

Tabaco The wooden tube used by the Carib Indians to inhale tobacco smoke. Europeans used this word for the plant itself.

PICTURE CREDITS

◄ I N D E X ►

P

Panama Canal 45
Pan-American Health Organization 19
plant life 24
population 48
postal system 85
Powell, Henry 31
Powell, John 31, 32
Prescod, Samuel Jackman 43, 58
Psychiatric Hospital 76

Q

Queen Elizabeth Hospital 76

R

revenue 67
Rights of Passage 60

S

St. Ann's Fort 83
St. George Valley 22
Saladoids 3
Salkey, Andrew 59
Samuel Jackman Prescod Polytechnic 81
Sandiford, Erskine 67
School for the Deaf and the Blind 80
School for the Mentally Retarded 80
Schoolmaster, The 59
slavery 18, 37
   end of 41–42
Spanish Main 30

sugarcane 34, 37
sugar plantation 39

T

tabaco 30
temperature 15
tobacco 17, 24
tourism 19, 70
Trafalgar Square 44
transnational corporations 72
"transportation" 34
Tumatumari 60

U

United Nations 18
University of the West Indies 19, 81

V

Visitor, The 85
Voice of Barbados 85

W

Walcott, C. L. 48
Weekes, Everton 48
Welchman's Hall Gully 83
West Indies 15, 21
World Bank 19
Worrell, Frank 48

Z

Zellers, Margaret 83